ARROWHEART
VOLUME I

"Write from the heart and aim for the truth."

Contents

"Curtains"
by Cat Halvorson

"The Mirror"
by Rachel Hutzenbiler

"Feigned Purity"
by Rob Kershner

"Salsify"
by Jill Koenigsdorf

"Rear View"
by Denise McCabe

"The Quickening"
by Caroline Smith

FORWARD

ArrowHeart Publishing is excited to present our debut collection of short stories! We started this press with the goal that we'd promote and collect valuable poems and stories from authors who vary in style, tone, and narrative structure. We're proud to say this volume does just that.

Naturally, having our deadline for submission for this volume in October, we received darker stories that leaned into the horror and suspense genre and that's fine by us! In the following pages, you'll find thrilling tales perfect for the spooky season with some varying genres sprinkled in.

For us, variation is key. We want diversity in both the types of stories we publish and the authors who created them. That mission is far from over. We are reaching out in the hopes of attracting more BIPOC and LGBTQ+ authors in our future volumes.

It is our firm belief that no matter who you are and what you like to read, you can pick up one of our volumes and find a story that resonates with you. We've been thrilled with the authors who submitted this year and encourage those who were not selected to submit again. ArrowHeart produces several volumes a year to give writers' their best chance at publication.

Now on to the future. This was our first volume and being our debut we didn't set down a theme in order to give our writers the upmost freedom. We still want to offer that freedom but feel that a slight nudge toward a centralized theme might help us reach and gather a wider range of authors. Not to mention, it will help our readers know what they'll be investing in from volume to volume. Our next ArrowHeart volume's submission deadline will be May 15, 2023. The theme for this collection will be "*IDENTITY*". Look to our website for more information on what that means at www.arrowheartpublishing.com.

To my writers, thank you for sharing your work and we can't wait to see what you do next.

To our readers, thank you for supporting the art of the short story, for taking in these narratives, and supporting our dream.

Happy reading!

-Dylan Ritch

Trigger Warning

ArrowHeart is committed to telling stories that come from the heart and aim for the truth of imagined human experience. That truth can contain unpleasant and unsettling thoughts and although that can resonate for many readers, for others it is harmful.

To navigate this issue with respect and compassion, we include a trigger warnings before every story. Our editor reads each piece and does their best to pull out the most prevalent trigger warnings. That way, you can skip any stories that may be harmful to your mental health. We apologize for any triggers we may have missed. Thank you for your understanding.

"Curtains"
by
Cat Halvorson

Trigger Warnings: Consent, Feeling unsafe in a Domestic relationship

Author Bio

Hailing from the Pacific Northwest, CL Halvorson is an upcoming writer of fantasy, horror, and surreal fiction, with occasional forays into other genres should the impetus strike. A victim of wanderlust, Halvorson seeks to explore both the waking and dreaming worlds and, through these experiences, weave tales that will inspire others in the ways they have been inspired. Their dearest wish is to have wings. To learn more about CL Halvorson, look to their upcoming website, liminallines.com.

CURTAINS

Exposition

When I woke, it was the colors that stayed with me. They were vivid, unsettling. Much like the dream itself.

I wasn't afraid. Though my dreams were frequent, vibrant, and often uncomfortable, they rarely scared me. Maybe because I usually knew I was sleeping. I tended towards lucid dreaming, and could sometimes even take control, like the director of a play - changing the backdrops, directing the players, redoing scenes that did not satisfy. Even when I wasn't in control, I still usually *knew* I was dreaming; knowing they weren't real kept the dreams from being truly frightening.

But this one was different. It was more than usually wrong, and though I could control my own actions, I hadn't realized it was a dream till the very end.

Rise

There was a murderer on the loose. What were the particulars? I didn't know, but someone had been doing horrific things. People were dying, and no one knew how to stop it.

I was approaching someone's home. In the dream I knew him, or was getting to know him, and I had come to visit. His house was white. The sun made it whiter. I climbed two or three steps to a small porch, and the door was open for me. Hanging in front of it was a red curtain.

No, not quite a curtain - more like a mobile, twisting from the hook above, dripping and oh so red. It was made of flesh, great swaths of skin hanging from fishing line. Someone had been flayed, the skin torn into pieces and strung up in the doorway. The face twisted with the other pieces, a gaping mask, and I could see through the eyeholes and sagging lips.

In my dream I knew, *I knew*, that the man who had done this was the man I had come to see. I side-stepped the grisly display nonetheless.

Climax

I was in his living room. The flesh curtain was gone now, but it was the same building, because the door looked out on the same porch, and anyway, I knew.

The room was white inside as well, illuminated by brilliant streams of sunlight. The windows were packed with plants. No flowers, just bright, lustrous leaves - hanging at various levels, nestled on the windowsill, a curtain of green drinking in the light.

I was tending to the plants. Walking along the verdant display, pressing my finger into the soil, watering the ones that were dry. Some grew in jars or glasses, their roots coiling in water instead of soil, and I had only to add fresh. My fingernail was black with dirt. I was helping my lover take care of his plants.

Fall

I stood in a dim and crowded room. My lover was showing me pictures from calendars filled with beautiful scenery. All the places we would see together, he said, as soon as I returned. I was leaving for a little while, I supposed, or perhaps I only had a short errand. In any case, I wanted - *needed* - to leave. I looked at the pictures he showed me and knew that I never wanted to be in any of those places with him.

But he couldn't know that.

I looked at him. He was not young, or particularly handsome. His face was narrow, his body thin - but he possessed a wiry strength, and his devotion to me was intense. I was his. I no longer wanted to be, but if he knew that he'd never let me go. Even if I did get away now, how could I keep him from finding me? He would follow. He'd never stop.

He turned from the pictures, all attention on me now. He held my hand up high, led me next to the bed. Not wanting to see my face, he kissed my knuckles instead, before spinning me around and holding me from behind. I kissed his forearm and let him pull me close.

He had an erection, I could feel it through my jeans. I had to get out. I felt myself leaning away from him and hoped he wouldn't notice, or if he did he would only think that I wanted to be on my way.

Not that I wanted to crawl out of my skin.

I felt his length press against me and thought again of that bright red curtain, dripping in the sunlight.

Catastrophe

That was when the dream began to fade. Waking was like floating to the surface of a bog, and my skin was heavy with the scum of it. The colors had been so vivid... I wanted to forget.

But I knew I wouldn't.

Not long after, I walked with a friend down an unfamiliar street. My companion knew a man, new to the neighborhood, who was having some people over. Not many. He didn't have a lot of friends here yet. It was something he and I had in common. According to my friend, we had many things in common, the host and I. We could be good for each other.

Then we turned the corner, and I saw.

I saw the porch, small and empty and pale. The curtain of green inside the windows. The setting sun painted the glass with red.

A familiar face opened the door and smiled at my companion. Then he looked at me, and I saw his eyes change. As if he recognized me too.

My steps did not falter, though they felt heavy.

I stepped inside. He closed the door behind me.

"*The Mirror*"
by
Rachel Hutzenbiler

Trigger Warnings: Excessive Alcohol Consumption

Author Bio

Rachel Hutzenbiler is a current graduate student living in the deserts of Arizona where she is studying Theatre for Youth and Communities. Writing has become a nice getaway from the studying life, a way to connect back to herself and re-center. Hutzenbiler's writing is strongly rooted in self and dreams, believing that the best stories are already living within and are just waiting to be told.

THE MIRROR

"Come."

I bolted upright from my bed, that scratchy, croaking voice pulling me once again from the void of dreamless sleep.

There.

In the corner by my cracked bedroom door, the pale light from the kitchen casting a shadow behind it. The creature was crouched this time, huddled in the shadow, one arm closed around its knobby knees and the other lightly placed on the door. The luminescent eyes of green, small beacons in the darkness.

"Come," it commanded again.

The eyes widened, staring at me intently.

"Not tonight. Please, just let me sleep."

I laid back down and turned away from it.

Momentary silence.

"Comeeeeee!"

The sound came from a new direction. I opened an eye and jolted, those green eyes mere inches from me. I knew better than to argue with it. Arguing never worked, just made it more insistent.

"Alright, alright!"

I pulled myself from the hug of my bed, wrapping a blanket around my bare shoulders. The creature, hunkering, opened the door and stepped beyond the threshold, looking back at me, expecting.

"What am I going to see tonight?" I asked, hopeful.

Silence. Only a hollow hand beckoning.

I hadn't really expected an answer. I followed the creature as I had many nights before, stepping beyond the threshold of the safety of my bedroom.

I hated this part. The world shifted, wobbled, nauseatingly spinning. I closed my eyes against the swirls and sworls. When I felt cold glass beneath my feet I opened my eyes.

The Other was the same as it always was. Black glass and black beyond. A strange light illuminating and casting shadows off the doors. Rows of doors framed the lines of a black hallway, each door dark wood and ominous. I never knew what I would find behind them when I looked. Happy memories, sad memories, funny ones. Memories of safety or heartbreak. Sometimes people I could barely remember would be waiting to be reintroduced. One time I discovered a memory of skipping across a creek, bare feet on warm stone, the water cool when my toes brushed its surface. Behind another door was a dead rabbit in spring green grass, its head far from its body. The blood bright against the white and gray fur.

The creature was moving down the invisible black hall, the endless doors rising up as it approached.

"Come," it commanded, its green tinged scales reflecting into the black glass.

I called it my creature, my gremlin, even my chaos at times, although I didn't believe it was a manifestation of myself. More of a messenger of the mind. The creature knew when it was time for me to remember, even if I didn't want to. As if the doors whispered to it before it came to wake me from sleep.

So I followed. I knew it was the only way to get back to that dreamless sleep. Simply follow and wait for one of the doors to whisper to me. Doors upon doors. Never ending. Each guarding a memory locked away. I had tried occasionally to open a door that hadn't whispered to me, but the door had refused my entry, locking the memory away even deeper.

There.

The creature stopped a few paces earlier, turning to me, questioning if I heard the whisper. I nodded and slowly approached. The door was just like all the rest, imposing and strong, giving no hint as to what it hid. I walked around it, hoping I would be given a clue. A hint. Anything. The door only whispered louder, annoyed it was being left waiting.

I sighed, then touched the doorknob. The door swung open soundlessly.

My childhood living room. The clock on the VCR read 12:46am. The room was exactly as I remembered it to be. The cream carpet, speckled with blue, stained in places from muddy shoes, spilled drinks, and adventurous children. The red walls with the white trim. Blue plaid armchair in the corner with the gold floor lamp behind it. I heard the burble of the fish tank, its light casting a strange, cool hue throughout the room. Wooden entertainment center with the doors open, the TV on, playing a late night Western movie, the sound so low it was barely audible.

I knew this memory. I knew what I would find behind me, on the plaid couch. I turned from the TV.

It was the bottles I saw first. A collection of them, shoulder to shoulder like little soldiers. One sat away from the rest, only half finished. An arm hung over the side of the couch, the bottle just out of its reach. I couldn't bring myself to look at the face of the sleeping man. Just as I had as a child, I stooped to pick up the bottles, the smell of cheap, stale beer biting into my nose. I carried them into the kitchen, and quietly deposited them into the recycling bin in the side closet, carefully, not wanting to wake the rest of the house.

There were flowers on the kitchen table. I hadn't remembered them as an adult. But mom always tried to keep flowers in the house, to bring some life and color into our lives. The same reason she gave us bright orange and purple and blue towels. Why every room in the house was colorful and patterned. Purple swirls, textured yellows, speckled blues.

An attempt at joy. Life.

The creature looked at me, the TV movie reflecting in its green eyes.

"Why?" I asked, keeping my back to the man, my voice barely above a whisper.

"Come," it responded, shuffling away.

I looked back at the scene in the room, turned off the TV, and followed the creature, the snores of the man following behind me.

The snores cut off with the click of the door.

"Come."

Silently the creature and I continued down the hall, waiting for the whispers. The only sound was the twinned padding of bare feet against glass, one set shuffling, the other even and heavy.

The whispers came from the left this time. The door was the same, waiting, impatient, imposing.

I silently begged it to be something happy, something far removed from the scene I had just left. I took a breath, reached out, and, just as before, the door opened silently under my touch.

The door slammed behind me as I ran down the front walk of the house to the waiting car. It was dark, so dark, only the pale yellow of the lamp lights shining to break that darkness. The daffodils were blooming, their cheerful yellow oddly sickly in the blanket of night.

The back door of the van was already open, waiting, an invitation. I jumped the flowers, running through the grass, begging to be in the safety of the car. I pulled myself into the seat, the tan fabric soft under my legs and hands. Something cold was put into my hands. Chocolate chip cookie ice cream. It tasted ashy in my mouth. I closed my eyes to the woman in the front door, watching, silhouetted by the light in the kitchen.

I knew the moment she turned away the yelling would start. An upbeat song began to blast through the car, barely deafening the pounding of my heart in my ears.

The van door slid closed with a click.

Silence.

My feet felt glass again. I opened my eyes and was no longer in the van, but looking at the wooden door in The Other.

"Come."

I obeyed, too tired to respond.

We walked and walked and walked. No more whispers came. Some nights it was one memory, sometimes three. One night I had been given seven. I had been a mess by the time I was brought home, overrun by forgotten moments.

A door at the end of the hall rose up before us. I had never been this far down the hall, never known it could end.

The creature grunted at me, nudging me forward with a bony finger. I walked through the door and discovered a room of black glass. A mirror of black obsidian rested before me, casually daring me to come closer.

To…

"Look," the creature guttered, pointing at the mirror.

"What will I see?"

"Look!"

I stepped forward cautiously, scared of what I might see. My reflection stepped forward with me, we stared at each other, waiting. I looked closer at myself. In a word, I was glorious to look at. Hair dyed too many times to be healthy, curly and wind swept, falling to proud shoulders holding my body tall. Commanding. Hands made to build and paint and create. To guide and teach. There was life in those eyes. So much life. They sparkled with laughter, curiosity and wonder, bright as the flowers on a table in a dark house.

I saw deeper into the reflection to the soul. Sure there were shadows haunting and creeping in the corners, but the soul shone bright, pressing the darkness to the very edges. Demanding them back. Despite everything.

How?

The reflection smiled softly at me, shrugging a non-committal answer. We continued to look at each other, slowly understanding, slowly learning. Memories behind unlocked doors working together to form the reflection I examined. Understanding that who I am wasn't built in a day.

"Thank you," I whispered to myself. "Thank you for being strong."

My reflection smiled again, walking away from the mirror, not before giving me a playful wink and a peace sign.

I turned to the creature waiting behind me.

"Come, I understand."

"Learning," it responded, the cracking voice soft.

So we left The Other, silent and pondering. A little wiser. A little stronger. Understanding more.

Across the threshold and back.

And the doors in The Other waited.

"Feigned Purity"
by Rob Kershner

Trigger Warnings: Suicide

Author Bio

The author has opted out of submitting a bio. We hope you enjoy their story!

FEIGNED PURITY

An outsider would mistake the scene in front of me for a path of the dead. In some ways it is: the penetrating cold, the unapologetic colorlessness, the nonsensical pureness of it all. My head spins, as if considering such a metaphor produces the only heat in my dreary body whilst it trudges through the snow... *Crunch, crunch, crunch.* It is the only sound I hear for hours – days – at a time, only interrupted by the occasional tumbling of the snow from the high branches as the trees mock me and my struggle against a villain that they can just shrug off. But I trudge on; it's all I can do.

For most of the time I spend on this road, the howling wind is my only companion. The ears of my younger self would have complained about our uninvited guest; now, though, my ears don't dare to air out their frustrations – they, at least, aren't the ones who have to march against the wind, are they?

In the distance, my tired eyes make out what is essentially a speck on the horizon. And at first, that's all I chalk it up to be: a distant, unimportant speck. After all, what would my eyes know anyway? They spend their countless hours staring at white nothingness. Not even the snow-covered trees offer any reprieve. *I'm* the one who navigates our path – my eyes are just getting a free ride.

After pushing forward just a bit longer, my nose begins to pitch in to the unwelcome intervention. I cross my eyes briefly -- though my legs don't let me take a break -- and I stare at the red blotch that partially impedes my eyes' sorry vision. My nose tells me that it smells smoke. *What would you know about smoke?* I ask harshly. *You've been numb for miles. What's given you the right to wake up now?* But, despite my pride, I am swiftly proven wrong. The speck isn't a speck: it's a man. And the smoke bellows not from my nose's false pretenses, but from the man's torch. I nearly halt in my tracks, but the hungry cold reminds me to move.

Spotting a traveler isn't new to me. I see them every now and again. And sometimes, ironically enough, they see me too. Most of the time -- whether it's caused by shame or guilt, I'm not sure – they keep their eyes down as we pass. Most of the time, the travelers in which I share a road pretend that my footsteps are cracking snow patches caused by the heat of their torch. I never hold these travelers' instincts against them. After all, if I were lucky enough to carry a torch like them, to wear warm clothing like them, to be able to feel my fingers like them, then I'd probably treat someone like me the same. What does someone have to gain from greeting me when they already have all a man could want?

But sometimes – *rarely* – travelers look at me. Their brown eyes pierce straight through to the very center of my gray corneas. And for a brief moment I too feel the warmth of their torch, almost as though they put it in my fist. These kinds of travelers never stop at simple eye contact. They always give one quick, decisive nod as if their acknowledgment of my mere existence is somehow a public duty that they alone fulfill. And the saddest part is that they're right.

I find myself wondering what kind of traveler this speck will be. Though, before my thoughts can once again warm my head, the cold slaps me. It knows where my mind goes when my path finally crosses with an interruption to the vast sea of nothing. And it scolds me. It tells me that the hope for eye contact, the hope for the nod, the hope for recognition is a burden. This traveler doesn't walk the same path as I do. No one does. So why should he have to fall victim to it as well? Why should he be force fed a taste of the frostbite when his torch – not the wind – is his companion?

Slowly, the deafening sound of my footsteps combine with his. But as if it's a mirror that I march past, I keep my head held low. My burden is my burden alone.

Soon enough, the *crunch*ing reverts to the familiar. And I, like most times, am death's only traveler. The wind circles, trying to distract my mind from its feeble hope. The wind reminds me of the road that lay ahead. It reminds me that I alone can walk it. And that the others that travel on it always travel in the opposite direction.

Soon enough, however, another speck decorates the thinly-veiled horizon. Though this time, the smoke that is born from the speck does not originate from a wealthy man's torch: it comes from a chimney. As my legs drag me closer, I can begin to make out the individual bricks that line its walls. Once I get even closer, the glass window transforms into a portal that leads to a world in which the wasteland I travel does not yet exist.

I watch a girl stand at a dark wooden table. Her long, black hair keeps getting in the way of her chopping. I smile, envious of her frustration. She moves her hair out of the way, and I tremble. She has no road to walk, no cold to battle, but instead, a simple flick of her wrist. She turns to face towards me, towards the one-way glass that I desperately peer through. The wind tugs at my arm, urging me to return my focus to the trek, but for the first time I dismiss it, opting to stare at the girl's familiar face. She sits on a cream sofa, and next to her is a man…

I shiver. Next to the girl is me.

She smiles nervously, like our 50th date is our fourth. "I hope the food comes out alright."

I smile in return. "I'm sure it'll be fine. I have faith in my sous chef."

"Oh, *sous* chef, huh?" She hits me for my teasing, and I *feel* her hit me. I *feel* the warmth that she creates. No longer am I on the road but I am next to her. I stare into her eyes, not for the need for recognition but because I *can*. Because I am there. Because I am not a burden to her. Nor am I an obligation. I am a person. A person who deserves to be cooked for. A person who deserves love. A person who deserves her.

Suddenly, though, I shiver. And she sees me shiver. And the smile evaporates from her face. And she retreats from the couch. And I was never good enough for her – I never deserved her. And just as quickly as her warmth became mine, her warmth disappeared. And now I find myself in the embrace of the cold, staring into a life that will not welcome me back. At least, not as easily as the wind does.

My legs start again, their rip cord being pulled by the ice: the same ice that tries to prevent their gears from turning in the first place. I follow my legs as the wind begs me to forget the window, the chimney, the warmth. But how can I forget? That was once mine. *She* was once mine.

And yet, the wind lectures, *Here you remain. On a frozen road, pining for the things that sit worlds behind you.*

My legs lead me forward, never daring to turn around. My nose, eyes, ears, and even my late fingers all know that this is for the best, as it's best not to pretend that turning around is as simple of an option as is what color shirt to wear in a world without color.

Suddenly, as though my thoughts had wandered down to my legs, I stop moving. At first, I scold my legs, but my eyes take their side and urge me to look forward. In front of me is a cliff that stretches so deep, not even the wind can travel to the bottom. I stand still, staring towards the magnificent end. Is this it? Does the road cease here? If it's meant to, then where's my torch? Where are my warm clothes? Where do I get the supplies to turn around and join the rest of my fellow travelers on the path back towards happiness?

Then it hits me: this cliff isn't something that all those other travelers had to see. As the realization sets in, the wind snickers. It knew that the cliff is what I had been marching toward. It knew this entire time. And deep down, I knew it as well. I knew that I would never escape the cold to suddenly find myself embraced by the warmth. After all, warmth isn't something that we all deserve. She showed me that. And since that day where I was forced to leave our house and leave our chimney, I knew that my new path – the annoyingly *crunch*y, bitter road – would lead me right here. After all, the road was never just a thing to be walked.

"Will you stay with me?" I ask, breaking the long silence.

Yes, the wind replies. *To the very end.*

My nose exhales, as if it too knows that the wind lies. But my eyes close anyway. And with a violent push, the wind and I find ourselves falling, falling, falling.

Even after the wind leaves my side, and it is just me descending towards the end, I smile, not out of happiness, but relief. Because, after enduring the impossibly cold road for years, I know that finally, within the span of one brief moment, I will be warm once again.

"Salsify"
by Jill Koenigsdorf

Trigger Warnings: Death

Author Bio

Jill Koenigsdorf is a writer and floral designer living in Sonoma, California. She is the author of the novel Phoebe and the Ghost of Chagall (MacAdam Cage 2012) Her short fiction has been published in ZYZZYVA, The Chautauqua Review, American Short Fiction, and others, and her stories have been nominated for a Pushcart Prize. Her non-fiction has appeared in many newspapers and magazines in The Bay Area and New Mexico. She is currently working on a new novel and a poetry collection.

SALSIFY

Sometimes, I forget where the bees end and I begin. I have made a place for myself in front the hives, eye level, tree stump chair, moss cushion, but I roll it away, back into the woods after each telling session so no one knows I've been there. I was spying upon Father from behind the lilac bush. I had heard him confess long ago that he wished he had Mother all to himself, that my brothers and sisters and I were *a nuisance* and *his downfall* and *a bane.* The lilac bushes formed a living wall that divided the orchards from our house, and they were near enough to the hives that when the blossoms were full of bees, when I used them for cover, the vibrations of the bees' wings would tickle the blonde hairs on my cheek. I had to keep myself from giggling. I had observed everyone in the family telling the bees their secrets. Sometimes they would lower their voices as if they were reliving the sin, and I had to strain to hear its nature. This was wrong of me I know, but it provided me a touchstone, a strand of kinship in a family so somber and pinched. And too, there was a softness in their telling that I rarely saw around our house, an openness. It made me like them all a bit better. Mother was different though. Mother was the one who brought joy.

Some of the neighbors only told their bees of monumental things, births and deaths, but my family worked things out in front of the hives, wrestling with longing and anger and shame, deep in that tug-of-war between failure and pride, desire and restraint. We all asked for signs from the bees, wanting to believe that they might somehow be able to communicate solutions. Father gulps frequently and worries his big hands in the telling, those hands not good for much besides working and hitting. I had to be very careful eavesdropping on Father, like a lacewing that thieves bugs already trapped in a spider's web, trying not to get caught in the web herself.

I watched Mother too, when still she lived, avidly telling the bees of her yearning for something beyond the drudgery of the orchard. She would sigh, her shoulders dropping, then bow her head in shame for having such selfish thoughts. Still, I noted, a half-smile played at the corners of her lips even in repentance, as if the small wickedness of stating a true desire aloud was rejuvenating. After her telling, she would thank the bees for carrying off her burdens by singing to them, some of the same songs she sang to me, *Lavenders blue, dilly-dilly/Lavenders green,* and each time she came to the *dilly-dilly* part, the golden ones would hover near her, making only soft sounds, like purring, lingering, as we all did, to hear her beautiful voice. All of my brothers and sisters had stern, bible names, Faith, Abraham, Neriah, names my Father chose. But Mother named me Salsify, after the flower whose root we ate to keep us healthy. *Easy and useful, pretty in its own way,* was how she put it, her reason for giving me that flower name. Then she added, *and the seeds, they are able to float far away.*

It was important to be respectful of the hives, to approach humbly, then tap once with a special stick to let the bees know we wanted counsel or had some important news. My brother Jacob had made our hives, with ingenious stacks of removeable drawers. We tapped with the special wand he had carved from the wood of one of the oldest Seek-No-Further apple trees in the orchard. This let the bees know that one of us was there, ready to begin. Jacob had carved the image of a Queen on the handle so true and detailed it even showed the tracery of her wings. Mother marveled, joking that we might wake up one morning and find that it had up and flown away. Jacob had beamed that day under the rare praise, but father told him straightaway to fetch some water and tossed the staff roughly in the corner, as if it were ordinary kindling. I cringed to hear it clatter on the floor.

Today the hives are covered with black muslin mourning cloth to let any passerby know that we have had a death in the family, though passerby are a rarity indeed in these parts. The bees go about their work, slipping into the hives underneath the hems of the shrouds, but I can tell they are affected by Mother's death too, their hum softer, their foraging flights less frequent. I am the youngest, three older brothers, three older sisters. Mother used to hold me close when we were alone at the well or at the clothesline and whisper, *The others were just practice,* and then she would make a shush sound, her finger to her lips. *You and I, Salsify, we're the wild ones,* and it was true. After that, I too had a secret, gift and burden both. But now only the constant sadness of no longer being anyone's favorite.

None of us much bothered with bee bonnets, nor any sort of defense, though we all knew how to use the smoker, working the bellows to lull them so we could take their honey. Mother always told us to leave some honeycomb in the box to feed the hive, at least two trays, especially in the

Fall and Winter, but Father took as much as he wanted, seeming to know the bare minimum the bees would need to survive. When I stared daggers at his back he sensed it and, without turning around, would say *Don't you look at me like that. This honey is part of what puts food in your belly and shoes on your feet.* Everyone knew he had eyes in the back of his head, but I was the one who could watch him in his tellings without him ever catching on. One time he admitted that he read the parables contained in the family bible but was uncertain of their meaning. Yet he insisted that children know them, back to front and 'round again.

The day Mother was buried, I stopped speaking, and have not spoken aloud to another in my family since. After the first week of my muteness, I heard Father talking low with the others that I was too young to understand her passing, that it would be up to my siblings to comfort me because *she's as peculiar as a six-toed deer and she don't ever pay no nevermind to anything I have to say.* He was wrong about me not understanding what death was. I had seen many deaths in the forest. Hatchlings carried off in the claws of ravens, the mother birds so tiny and desperate, chasing and pecking at the fleeing marauders to no avail. Calves and foals stillborn, perfect, motionless and new. Rabbits and squirrels who had frozen in the winter. Mother said freezing was a peaceful way to die. I have witnessed murder too, the work of yellowjackets, the enemy of all bees. They will stop at nothing to get into the hives, eating everything, the larvae, pupae, the honey, flinging the bees on the ground and stinging them dead. It seems unfair that the wasps can sting as many times as they choose, and just fly off, while the bee must consider carefully, knowing it will lose its life after it stings.

All of us have been stung a few times, and it hurts sure, but more I feel sorry for the bee. They think only of the hive, giving their life to protect it. Mother taught us to just put some honey on a sting, surprising us with the strange, circular wonder that both the cause of the pain and the cure for it, were made by the bees. She says being stung make us resistant to ailments. Yet, incredible to think about now, Mother was the only one who had never been stung, the one who gathered honey without the smoker, cooing and saying sweet things to the honeybees just like she did to the chickens when she gathered eggs. Father said bees can smell fear, like dogs, but that makes no sense, because she and I were not afraid at all that day. We were laughing, quietly of course, and we both wore the clover crowns I had made for us earlier, making our way past through the wild blue Chicory and down to the hives. I won't allow myself to consider that my clover crown might be the very thing that drew the bees stronger to her face, for that brings on a woe too crushing for me to bear. It all seems like long ago now, yet still a fresh torment each day. I was with her when she got stung. I had joined her to help, but instead I watched her die. I did not know what to do.

I followed after her that morning with a bucket for the comb and honey, happy it was just us two. She always let me chew on pieces of the comb and that was a favorite thing. It was late Summer, the apples green on the trees, but the fields near water still full of blossoms dizzying fine, each containing their own bee. Father says all bees look the same, but he is wrong. I had favorites and could tell them apart, a particular worker with his pollen pantaloons and his crooked antennae, I named him Loyal, him always the first one out in the mornings, and the last one back in. The fuzziest of all the bees, I called him Trueheart. Mother was singing that morning as she worked, and her lips must have been parted just enough, and the bee must have been in a gathering frenzy and just flew right into her mouth by accident and stung her. She spat furiously, like she had eaten something nasty, and waved her hand frantically in front of her face, from the shock of it, never having been stung, and too because no doubt it hurt. After that, everything slowed down around us. Something switched in her expression, bewilderment, and then I watched her drop hard onto her knees like someone had commanded her to kneel. Her face slackened and she looked confused. *Mother?* I called out, running towards her. But she fell further, her cheek in the dirt now. *Mother? Mother?* I was screaming now. I did not know what to do. *Tell me what I should do, Mother oh please! Tell me!* I sat alongside her and lifted her head onto my lap, and she stared up at me, unseeing, bubbles of foam forming in the corners of her mouth. I started to rock her desperately. She spasmed like a fish on shore, and I stroked her hair, over and over, knowing I should be doing something more, but not wanting to leave her. Nor did I know what to say except for *shush shush now now there there.*

Then, things happened too fast. Her tongue swelled up to the size of a yam. She convulsed again and became heavy in my lap. She could not breathe right and made gasps that terrified me. *I'll go get Father. Should I go get Father? Can you hear me? I'll be back, Mother, I swear it!*

When I finally reached someone, my brother Jacob, I discovered I could not make a sound, I could only mime for him, wringing my hands, pointing and running towards where she lay. I would surely shatter if I heard the unbearable, that final edict, so once Jacob was close to her, I

30

held back, watching from behind a tree. By now the whole family was running towards her, but I saw she lay unmoving, her neck and cheeks horribly swollen, purple. Father knelt and shook her, hard, then wailed and lifted her to him, rocking her as I had done, but she was gone. My siblings backed away from him, for he was mad with grief or rage, we did not know which. He saw me then, and strode towards me, a giant who yanked me from my hiding place and slapped me across my face, yelling *what did you do to her? What did you do?* I could not speak but I did not flee, for my answer was also my guilt. *Nothing.* I wanted to tell him. *I did nothing.* He pushed me from him, offering no comfort to any of us, and as he passed the hives, he kicked at one of them. The bees, betrayed, swarmed around their fallen home, immediately setting about trying to repair the damage. Honey spilled from the opening like blood from a deep wound.

It is harvest time now, for the early crops, the Bevan's Favorites and Black Limbertwigs, and we are grateful for the escape of hard work. There is no joy at our table, no song, the food bland and basic. Yesterday I found some cinnamon in the cupboard and after Father had left to tend the horses, I sprinkled it on each of my siblings' oatmeal. For the first time, Faith smiled, then around the table, one by one, we all did. A tiny thing, a small salvation. It is too oppressive inside for me, so I have become a feral thing. I sleep outside wrapped in mother's warm shawl, attuned to crickets at night and mourning doves at dawn. Everyone leaves me be.

Two weeks have passed since we buried her. We brought one of the hives down to the gravesite so the bees could witness, placing it upon a piece of fabric torn from one of her favorite dresses so they would not forget her. Last night, someone had lifted the black mourning cloth from the hives, as if it the tragedy was over or might ever be. And still I do not speak, except to the bees, privately when the others are in the orchard or getting supplies in town. My voice is hoarse, a rusty whisper. *Mother is gone,* I tell them again. *I do not blame you. She has already forgiven us all. She is happy now.* Maybe this is a lie, but a comfort also, perhaps more for me than the bees.

Today, during my telling, the bee with the largest eyes is poised right in front of my face, then so close to my ear its hum fills me, and I vibrate with it, a tuning fork. We look at one another for a good minute. I can see the tiny hairs on its shoulders, the dusting of yellow pollen on its abdomen. She lands on me, and I let her antennae appraise me as she crawls along my brow and down my cheek. Surely it is the same bee that hovered at mother's grave the day we buried her. They say when a bee appears at a funeral it is the deceased's soul leaving their body. Perhaps this particular bee is her, the one. As I imagine this, she flies off and merges with dozens like her. I follow them to the meadow, where the Salsify are still in bloom, even this late in the season. The bees move down their purple petals to work the heart, gathering, feeding, losing themselves in all but industry. And there at my feet is one Salsify that has already gone to seed. I pick this stem with its puffball head, take a magnificent breath, and blow. The feathered seeds dance before me and are blown away, all in different directions, light and indistinct, able to ride the wind, to land somewhere else, and then begin to grow.

"Rear View"
by Denise McCabe

Trigger Warnings: Death, Grieving

Author Bio

After working for WNEW Radio, International Creative Management, Time-Life Films, HBO, and as an independent theater agent in New York, Denise moved to Los Angeles and worked for several small film companies, coproducing several low budget films before deciding to stretch creatively and find her own voice as a writer.

She has since written over 30 short stories, several of which have been published, and one of which, Sophie, was a runner up in Narrative Magazine's spring fiction issue. A selection of her fiction, Flicks, was performed at the New Federal Bar in North Hollywood, California as part of their "New Short Fiction Series."

Visit her website at https://denise-mccabe.com

"REAR VIEW"

I saw Jimmy for the last time on a gloriously warm day in late winter, just after we turned the clocks ahead.

It was on that little curve of road where Holloway turns onto Sunset Blvd. I was waiting for the left turn arrow when I saw him walking West on the other side of the street. I couldn't see his face - his back was to me - but I recognized his bruised corduroy jacket and his baggy jeans, and of course his body was still unmistakeable to me even after being out of my sight for almost a year.

The light changed and the car behind me tapped on his horn to wake me up. I made the left onto Sunset, pulled over to the curb half a block past him and waited. I called out to him as he reached the passenger window and he turned as if startled to hear a voice. He bent down to look in the window and for an instant it seemed he didn't know me, but then I saw his face soften and he said my name.

"Where are you going?" I asked him.

It seemed to take him a beat longer than it should have to register my question. I wondered if he was medicated or suffering from some sort of medical condition. But his eyes were clear and his voice was strong when he answered that he was on his way to the Whiskey to interview for a possible gig.

"I'll give you a ride," I said.

It was only two blocks away, but he opened the door, tossed his duffel bag onto the floor, and climbed in. He smelt of cigarettes and loneliness.

"Nice car," he said.

"Still smoking I see."

"You know how it is."

I watched the road while he watched me. Thirty seconds later, I signaled and pulled up in front of the Whiskey. He put his hand on the door handle and waited.

"I hope you get the gig," I said.

"Thanks. It's a long shot, but that's all I've got left."

"Everything is a long shot. Buck up," I said.

He used to get angry when I'd hit him with my brand of tough love,

35

but not this time. He just looked over with weary eyes and tried to smile.

"I'm really sorry I haven't been in touch. It looks like you're doing well. I'm happy for you. You deserve it."

I wanted to ask him where he was staying but knew it wouldn't be smart to open up that line of conversation. I signaled and pulled over to the curb to let him out. He hesitated for a second with his hand on the door handle, then shot me a wink and a quick salute.

"See you on the radio," he said.

He picked up his duffel bag and got out of the car. I turned away, waited for a break in the traffic, and pulled out.

His name was Jimmy Peacock, at least that's the name he used professionally, except he never really settled on a profession. He was by his ever-shifting definition a musician, an actor, a writer, or anything that would inevitably doom him to failure and despair.

He was my father once, but that seemed as remote as if it had happened in a movie. Now he was just a casual acquaintance from the past who needed a shot at life. I had spent almost four years waiting for that shot with him; cheering him on; shouting at him; crying; wanting him to leave yet wanting him to stay. And then one day it was over. He packed up his few possessions and hired two day laborers from Home Depot to move what little he had into storage.

My mom died when I was fourteen. Jimmy tried to cope with me but his own failed dreams kept getting in the way. He waited until my eighteenth birthday so I was legally an adult and wouldn't have to go into the system. By that time, we were about to lose the apartment, and I couldn't have afforded the rent anyway, so I went to live with a friend whose parents had always treated me as their own daughter. They'd known what Jimmy was like, but never said a word against him. It was easy enough to read their thoughts.

I drove away without even a glance in the rearview mirror. For the rest of the day, thoughts of Jimmy cropped up, like grit in my shoes - uncomfortable, sometimes painful, but easy enough to shake out.
I had no reason for looking back, and no sympathy for anyone who mourned the past. As Jimmy had said in the car, I was doing well: making good money, driving a nice car, and living the good life in a beautiful apartment in the city of dreams. I didn't need anything from Jimmy or anyone else, so it was easy to push the regrets aside and just get on with it as I had always done.

A week later, I met Valerie.

*****

It was a Tuesday morning, a work day for me. I had just stepped out of the shower and I certainly wasn't expecting any visitors. I thought it might be Jimmy, as he had a habit of showing up whenever the mood suited him, usually at inopportune moments.

I put on my robe and looked through the peephole. It wasn't Jimmy, but an attractive woman in her forties. I opened the door.

"Are you Priscilla?" she said.

"Who are you?"

"Valerie. I don't know if your dad has told you about me."

"We don't speak much."

Silence.

"Are you his girlfriend?"

"I'm his wife."

"Wow."

"Do you mind if I come in?"

She looked around but seemed too nervous to focus on anything.

"Is this about Jimmy?"

"He hasn't been home for a few days and I'm worried."

"Disappearing is his specialty. He always comes back, so I wouldn't worry too much." Nothing could be gained by airing old grievances in front of this stranger who was, technically at least, my stepmother. She seemed way out of his class but I wasn't really surprised. Jimmy possessed a certain sexy, tortured quality that some women find irresistible. She wanted to save him. I wondered if she had yet realized he couldn't be saved.

"The most he's ever done is sleep in his car for a night, but he always comes back in time for coffee and a shower. This is going on three days. His phone goes straight to voice mail. I left a few messages but it's pretty clear he either can't or won't call me back."

"How long have you been married?" I said.

"It'll be a year in June."

She looked embarrassed, but of course it wasn't her fault. It also wasn't the first time Jimmy had taken a Sabbatical from someone's life.

"I have to get ready for work. I'm really sorry I can't help you. If you want to leave your phone number, I'll call you if I hear from him."

She fumbled in her purse and pulled out a business card. *Valerie Moffatt* it said, and under the name in bold letters **FACE FORWARD** and an address in Hollywood.

"What kind of work do you do?"

"I run a mentoring program for at-risk teenagers, helping them to stay in school, develop their talents, avoid getting into drugs or other trouble. That's what the company name is about: looking forward, not back."

"Very noble of you."

I realized after I said it that it sounded flip, but that wasn't my intention. The irony, however, was inescapable.

"I'm no Mother Theresa, believe me. I just came into some money and I wanted to put it to good use."

I put her card down on the coffee table and walked her to the door. She looked as if she wanted to give me a hug but thought better of it and held out her hand instead.

"I hope we can meet again under better circumstances," she said. I closed and locked the door behind her and got dressed for work. No word from Jimmy for over a year, and then suddenly he was back in my life like a bedbug. But not for long. The next time I heard from Valerie, it was to tell me Jimmy was dead.

*****

He was discovered slumped over the steering wheel of his car in the parking lot of the Norm's Restaurant on La Cienega. I really didn't feel anything other than a sense of finality. *That's that*, I thought. It wasn't that I didn't care. I'm not totally heartless, nor am I unforgiving. It's just that it was a fitting end for a man who refused to be ordinary. No grieving relatives at his hospital bed; no last rites; no reading of the will. Just a bus boy taking out the garbage in the back of a diner.

"I'm sorry for your loss," I told her.

"Thank you. I'm sorry for your loss too."

Her words surprised me. Jimmy had been lost to me for years. She said she would contact me about funeral arrangements and we said goodbye. The next day, she called and asked me to drop by her place after work. She lived in the Los Feliz area in a small but elegant home that must have cost a fortune.

Jimmy had certainly done well for himself. She gave me the obligatory tour and then took me into the living room and asked me to have a seat. She opened a closet and took out a beat up guitar case.

"Your dad wanted you to have this."

It was Jimmy's most prized possession, his Gibson twelve string guitar. He used to sing me to sleep at night when I was small, and taught me how to play chords as soon as I was old enough to hold it. I never pursued any kind of musical aptitude I might have had, not wanting my life to follow in his doomed footsteps, but I could still remember the songs: *A Horse With No Name, Early Morning Rain, Mr. Tambourine Man, Stairway to Heaven.* These were my lullabies.

"You should probably keep this, or give it to one of your students or mentees, whatever you call them. I don't play anymore."

"He made me promise I'd give it to you. He put it in his will."

"He had a will?"

"I know. It sounds ridiculous. He barely had cigarette money. But he was very specific about this guitar. I wouldn't feel right about taking it."

"Even when money was tight, which was almost always, he refused to pawn it. Said it would outlast him. Looks like he was right."

"All the more reason you should have it."

I stroked the beautiful wood and ran my fingers up and down its spine. But somehow I couldn't play a single chord.

"Do you want some tea? I was just about to make some."

We took our cups out on the terrace, and sat quietly, enjoying the unseasonable warmth of the late winter sun. I asked her if she and Jimmy had been happy together.

"There was a certain comfort and contentment. But I don't think happiness was in his nature. He was always grasping at something just out of reach. He believed that life had cheated him - that he was destined for greatness but it eluded him."

She refilled our cups. It was strong tea, freshly brewed, with real cream and sugar.

"This is good," I said.

"I believe that tea should be a ritual, not just something to drink."

"I grew up on Lipton."

"We all did."

It was comfortable sitting with her. She was quiet in the same way that I was; not feeling the need to speak just to spout words. After a while, she asked me about my mother.

"What do you want to know? She was great. Beautiful, funny, shy. She died too young."

"So did your dad."

"Yes."

"I was hoping you'd help me plan the service. He wanted to be cremated. He said he'd rather go up in flames than decay slowly."

"The rock 'n roll way."

"I guess you could say that, yeah."

*****

It was a strange memorial service. No casket, just an urn on a pedestal in the center of the room and a handful of scruffy looking souls I had never met going up to it as if following some pagan ritual. I sat next to Valerie wondering who these people were, what I was doing there, and how quickly I could escape.

Into this motley crew of anonymous vagrants came a woman not much older than I but looking like a relic of the nineteen sixties: long dark hair, maxi dress, pink-tinted glasses. She drifted past us and I caught the scent of patchouli as she made her way up to the urn. She bent down and touched it gently, as if it were a baby bird that had fallen from its nest. Then she knelt down on the floor and began to quietly weep.

"Who is that?" I whispered to Valerie. She looked at me.

"That's Anna. You never met her?" "No. Should I have?"

"She was a runaway, someone your dad met outside one of the clubs. She lived with him for several months I think, and then he brought her in to the program when he couldn't take care of her anymore. That was how Jimmy and I first met."

"She's too young for him."

"Oh it wasn't like that. She was more like a daughter. Oh my God, I'm so sorry."

My head felt tight and I needed to get out of the room. Valerie looked like she wanted to crawl under a rock.

"I need to find the ladies' room," I said.

I made it out to the parking lot and kept going. There was a Burger King on the next block and I went in and ordered coffee and a Whopper, hold the onions. I knew I'd never be able to eat anything but I felt embarrassed just ordering coffee. Stupid I know, but that's how I am. I sat at a table in that totally sterile and anonymous atmosphere drinking black coffee and for all the ferociousness of my emotions, I could not manage to shed a single tear.

"*The Quickening*"
by Caroline Smith

Trigger Warnings: Death, Possession

Author Bio

Caroline Smith graduated from Queens University of Charlotte with an MFA in Creative Writing and got her BA from Pacific Lutheran University in English Literature and a minor in Publishing and Printing Arts. While there she fell in love with editing manuscripts and storytelling. She is currently the CCO of Tandem Light Press and author of four books including her latest Southern Gothic short story collection, "Shadows in the South."

When she's not writing or editing, she enjoys reading romance novels and dark fantasy and dreams of living in Scotland. She lives on a small farm in North Georgia with her three wild and wonderful children and a menagerie of animals. Learn more at https://www.editorcaroline.com.

THE QUICKENING

"You work too much. Let's do something fun tonight." The voice on the other end of the phone complained.

"It's Monday," Constance was baffled at the suggestion and raised her eyebrows at the phone on her desk. Her fingers typed melodically on the keyboard in front of her.

"But it's a full mooooon," Kristin sang.

Constance rolled her eyes and glanced at the long list of deadlines that peppered her calendar. Her best friend wasn't wrong about her working too much lately. She spent more hours at her desk than anywhere else these days.

"What did you have in mind?" Constance knew she'd give in because she always did.

"There's this old church I've been wanting to take you to. It has a graveyard I think you'd like."

"That's a carrot to dangle if ever there was one."

Kristin chuckled. "I know. That's why I said it."

"You know, most women our age go to brunch to hang out or leave their kids at home for a spa weekend."

"Come on. You know damn well we're not like 'most women.' Let Lizzie put the kids to bed and we'll be home when we get home."

Constance stayed quiet. She hadn't actually said yes yet but getting out of the house seemed like it might be worthwhile. These four walls were starting to press in on her.

"You just said last week that you needed more writing inspiration. Consider this it."

Constance sighed, "All right. Give me ten minutes to wrap this up and grab some things."

"Perfect. I'll come get you. I don't even know how to tell you where to go."

Constance hung up the phone and called her daughter into her dimly lit office.

"Your aunt is taking me on an adventure…apparently."

Lizzie's tall frame leaned against the wall and her eyes went dramatically wide. "You're *actually* leaving the house?"

Constance chuckled. "Don't be so shocked."

"Mom, you seriously haven't been anywhere in months. I'm starting to worry that you're becoming a recluse."

Constance rubbed her face. "I know. I've just had a lot going on. It's late already and I don't know what time we'll be back."

"It doesn't matter. Just go. I'll put the heathens to bed. Where is she taking you anyway?"

"Some old church with a graveyard she wants me to see."

"Well, that's fun. You love a graveyard. But…" Lizzie pushed away from the wall and walked toward the organized chaos on her mom's desk. "Aunt Kristin does know that this gift you have isn't some sort of party trick, right?"

Constance swiveled toward her. "What do you mean?"

"This is the third time she's taken you somewhere to see if it's haunted. You're sensitive. Not some kind of…" she waved her hand in the air looking for the right term, "ghostly Geiger counter."

Constance smiled. "She knows that. I think it amuses her because she can't feel it as much."

"Remember last time? You were in bed for two days recovering from The Biltmore."

"Yes, well, I've learned my lesson since then. I'm not going unprepared this time. Will you bring me the pouch on my altar? I want to send one more email before we go."

One of Lizzie's eyebrows lifted in consternation then she pushed off the desk and made her way upstairs, "You work too much," she called from the landing.

As soon as she closed her laptop, the front door swung open and her pink-headed neighbor-turned-bestie walked into a room with an excited dog and children that screamed for hugs.

Constance lifted a corner of her mouth in amusement at the chaos.

"You ready?" Kristin peeked her head into the open doorway. "It smells like workaholism in here, by the way."

"So you and Lizzie keep telling me."

"I knew I loved that child for a reason," she grinned broadly.

"Yes, I'm ready."

Lizzie clomped down the stairs, pouch in hand. "Found it."

"Where are y'all going?" Grady, Constance's middle child and only son looked bewildered that his mom was leaving on a school night.

"Out," Kristin shrugged.

"Be good for your sister and don't forget to brush your teeth." Constance leaned down and rubbed her nose against his in what he called a "nose kiss."

"I won't. Sissy's going to let me play video games until bed. Right, Lizzie?" He waggled his eyebrows at her.

Megan tackled her mother in a hug. "Bring me something back."

"We're not going anywhere like that, but we'll see."

"I guess headstones are a little hard to get into the car."

Constance looked at her seven-year-old as her eyebrows shot up to her hairline. "How did you know we were going to a graveyard?"

Meg shrugged. "Just did. Come on, Lizzie! Let's go watch Bluey."

Lizzie allowed herself to be dragged back into the living room. "Bye, mom," she called.

"What's that?" Kristin asked as she and Constance walked to her car, nodding at the pouch in Lizzie's hand.

"Just some crystals and herbs."

They were mostly quiet on the drive, which was unlike both of them when they were together. Constance tried to rub away the bit of anxiety she could feel bubbling up in her chest.

"It won't be like last time," Kristin said gently.

"Probably not," Constance said with more confidence than she felt. "In my experience ghosts don't hang out in graveyards anyway. What made you pick this one?"

"I found a book in town on all of our local ghost stories. Something closer to home sounded like it might be fun. It's not so much the graveyard that I want to take you to, but the church."

"What about the church?"

"Apparently it was built in the late 1800s after the cemetery had already been there for a while. I don't want to give anything away, but there are supposed to be scratch marks on the walls inside. They tried to cover them up a while ago, but they just keep coming back." Kristin widened her eyes in mock terror. She loved anything having to do with horror.

"Haunted I will do, evil spirits not so much."

"I'm sure it'll be locked up anyway, but I want to see it. And I know how much you like old cemeteries."

45

"Usually during the day," Constance muttered to herself. She looked up at the full moon. No matter what else happened in her life, the moon was her constant. Her touchstone. Even on the nights that were pitch black when it was new, there was always the promise that it would return, bright as day within a few short weeks. She let the light of it wash over her through the open window and settle her nerves. *Mother goddess, give me strength. Keep us safe and protected.*

"What does William think of you doing this, by the way?"

Kristin snorted. "Please, he knows I'm safer with you than by myself. He's putting the boys to bed and crashing."

The road to the church took them through old mining roads and onto what had now become part of Chattahoochee National Forest. It wound around curves with old, sentinel pine trees keeping watch. Kristin's headlights shone on a sign as they turned the corner: Cane Creek Baptist Church 1.0 Mile.

"Wait. Is this church still having services?"

"Seems to be." Kristin turned the radio down as they got closer. "Are you nervous or intrigued?"

"Yes." Constance rubbed her thumb over the canvas pouch still in her hand. There were no streetlights around, but the shadows of the woods seemed darker than they had been a few miles ago. Maybe the trees were packed tighter here or maybe Constance's imagination was already running away with her.

The road turned to dirt, and they bumped along slowly until a white building appeared in a valley. It looked nothing like what Constance imagined it would. The building itself was wide with no steeple. No cross. There was nothing to distinguish it as a church at all. It looked more like an old one-room schoolhouse. There was no sign on the front of the church either. Just a date-stamp of April 28, 1866, on the siding under what she might call an attic window.

"Let's go to the cemetery first. That church gives me the creeps."

Kristin nodded and drove past the church on a narrow driveway that connected it to the cemetery in the back. Headstones large and small popped up from a hill that sat higher than the church below it. The long shadows behind them made them more ominous than they really were. The edges of the cemetery were enclosed from the rest of the world by more tall trees. If they hadn't been going up the driveway, Constance never would have even known it was there.

As they rounded a curve in the back, the unsettling feeling Constance always got when spirits were around started. This had happened so many times by now that she was easily able to identify it. She'd learned over the years that people seemed to be sensitive in different ways: clairvoyance, clairsentience, increased sensitivity to smells or sounds. Goosebumps that ran along the arms or a "pins and needles" feeling on the back of the neck. Her gift wasn't like that. The alarm started in her belly, which suddenly felt like it was stuffed with cotton balls, and a headache that wrapped around the crown of her head like thorns and tingled when she tried to concentrate on it.

"Stop here."

Kristin looked at her, stopped the car, and put it in park. "Already?"

Constance nodded and opened the door. To their left was a giant marble grave marker that towered over the rest. Constance walked over to it and ran her fingertips over the rough-aged stone. In the moonlight, she could make out a confederate cross on the top. The man here had been buried with his wife: The Bruce's. Their names were engraved on the back of the stone.

Kristin shone her red flashlight on the front. "Looks like he was killed in the war. The year says 1861."

Constance rubbed her fingers over the stone where the birth and death dates of the wife had been carved. Her hand recoiled when she did the same with the husband's. "How weird."

"What?" Kristen moved over to where she stood.

"Look at the stone. His death date has been covered."

Kristin shone her flashlight where Constance's fingers had just been. Over the death date was a piece of smooth marble that had been cut to fit over it. It hadn't been carved out, but it was erased just the same.

"I've never seen anything like that."

"Let's see if there are others like it."

They walked to the next set of headstones. These were normal in size, up to their knees. Another wife beside her husband. The wife's headstone was normal and her death date was listed as 1863, but the husband's was like the previous: a thin strip of marble had been attached to the death date to cover it.

What looked like a family cluster sat just behind them and they turned to investigate that one. There was an infant that had died at just three days old. Next to him was his sister who was only six according to her headstone. An older brother who'd died in 1860 at just fifteen, their mother had lived to be sixty-eight, but the father's age was again unknown. He'd been born in 1815, but like the other headstones, the date of his passing was a mystery.

A shiver ran up Constance's spine.

"I don't understand. Why go to all this trouble? And why is it only the men?"

"It can't be on all of them, can it?"

Kristin stood in place and beamed her flashlight over the closest headstones. On some, the white of the new marble that covered the death dates stood out; on others, it seemed as old as the original stone.

"This wasn't in the book?"

"No. It just mentioned that the cemetery had been here before the church was built." She wandered over to a headstone that looked newer. "Huh. This one has the date he died. June 24, 1978."

"So maybe it's just the older ones from the 1860s?"

Movement at the edge of the cemetery caught Constance's attention and she looked to her right. Set in the very back at the treeline was another small cluster of three headstones. These were almost overgrown in comparison to the well-manicured ones in the front.

Without saying anything to Kristin, Constance made her way slowly over to them, letting the moonlight guide her.

Something inside her told her that these stones, this family, was different.

She knelt in front of the three uniform headstones. They were large rectangles with angled fronts, but they were almost illegible. Constance pushed back the kudzu that was threatening to overtake the smallest of the three.

Infant, Born November 10, 1859 - Died November 13, 1859

"Another baby. It also only lived for three days. It doesn't even have a name."

"Here." Kristin pulled out the knife she always kept in her pocket and Constance went to work clearing away more kudzu and weeds from the other two headstones.

"Parents, I think."

Kristin kept the flashlight in place and then Constance leaned back to study the dates on them.

Garland Gooch, Born January 10, 1835 - Died August 18, 1859
Sarah Gooch, Born August 17, 1840 - Died November 19, 1859

"His date is here. He died while she was pregnant if my math is right. And she died a week after the baby died."

"That's so sad," Kristin said quietly.

Constance nodded. She reached out a hand to touch Sarah's headstone. *Emily.* The name whispered in her mind but held no meaning for her. "She was only nineteen. He was twenty-four."

The stuffy feeling in Constance's head and stomach receded a little bit. The stone under her hand warmed.

"Uh, Con…look."

Constance turned around to look in the direction that Kristin was turned and pointing her flashlight. A soft fog was beginning to creep toward them. It seemed to be emanating from the church.

"I'm not sure we're going to make it in there tonight, K. I think we need to go."

"You don't have to tell me twice."

Kristin practically sprinted back to her car. She had it started and in gear before Constance even reached her door handle.

"Come on, woman!" Kristin was clearly shaken. "I don't feel like being demon meat tonight."

"Go!" Constance said as she shut her door.

The gas pedal had never been so taxed as Kristin floored it around the rest of the roundabout and down the hill.

The fog had crept along the driveway and if it had been solid, it would have blocked them from leaving. Instead, Kristin drove straight through it without slowing. As she did, Constance felt a roaring in her ears, like a thousand bees were trying to make a home in her head. She covered her ears, but it was gone before they reached the end of the church parking lot. When she looked behind them, all she could see was the fog swirling and dissipating behind them.

The silence returned to the car as they caught their breath. Constance couldn't stop thinking about the Gooch family and their wooded mausoleum. She got the sense that the people that buried them wanted to forget them, but also give them a proper, Christian burial. She wanted to know more, needed to know more about what had happened to them.

"Well that was fun," Kristin said sarcastically.

"No joke. Can I just remind you that this was your idea?"

"I have bad ideas. You're supposed to tell me that going to a cemetery on a full moon is a bad idea. I'm the baby witch, remember? You're the one with the experience here."

"Yeah, but I've never seen anything like that. Haunted houses, spirits that appear to me, shifts in energy, dreams, sure. But not this."

"What was it?"

"I don't know." She paused, considering what she'd just seen. "But I want to."

"Well, I don't need to know anymore. If you come back here…ever… don't bring me."

"You aren't curious? About the dates that were erased off of all those headstones?"

Kristin glanced over at her. Her speed had gone back down to a moderate 35 mph to accommodate the curves of the mountainous roads.

"What *are* you talking about?"

Constance frowned. "What do you mean 'what am I talking about'? All of the headstones that we found who had no death dates."

"Did you hit your head getting back to the car?"

"Pull over."

"What d–"

"Just pull over."

Kristin found a gravel pull-off on the side of the road and pulled in.

Constance turned in her seat and adjusted her seatbelt to see her best friend better. Her hands were shaking, but if it was from adrenaline or the thought that Kristin didn't remember or know what they'd seen in the cemetery she didn't know.

"Tell me everything you remember from what just happened."

Kristin's brows furrowed as she looked at Constance. The glow from the lights on the dashboard showed Constance the sweat that beaded on Kristin's upper lip and brow. The same light twinkled off the pentagram that hung from Kristin's neck.

"We got to the cemetery, we looked around at the headstones. We saw the family in the back, we cut away the kudzu, the fog came, and…we left."

"You don't remember anything remarkable about any of the headstones?"

"Not really. There was that one tall one in the middle. We saw a few babies. I did think it was odd that the last family…the Gooch's, right?…were set so far away from all of the other gravestones."

Constance's mind reeled. How was this possible? They had discussed all of the missing dates. *Dammit, I should have taken pictures.*

She rubbed the space in the middle of her forehead trying to soothe the tension headache that was beginning.

"Okay. When we drove through the fog, did anything happen? Did you hear anything?"

Kristin looked confused. Her pink bob shook slightly as she slowly shook her head. "Hear anything? Con…are you okay? I'm seriously worried about you."

"Just tell me." Constance's voice was a little harsher than she intended, and Kristin shrank back as much as the car would let her.

"No. It was just fog. We drove through it. I didn't hear anything." Kristin rubbed Constance's arm. "I think we need to get you home. You look a little pale."

Constance sighed and turned back in her seat, resting her head against the headrest as her mind tried to process what had just happened. There was too much. The warming of the headstone she thought she understood. Sarah Gooch must have been the presence she'd felt. The fog and the headstones were another mystery that she'd have to unravel. Fortunately, she at least had an idea of where to start.

The next morning, after she'd taken the kids to school, she sat in the library parking lot waiting for it to open. Kristin had been texting most of the morning making sure she was okay. She tried to reassure her, but the lie of being "okay" felt heavy in her stomach.

She stared deeply into her black coffee, not really seeing it and not having the stomach this morning to even drink it. Something was off, but she didn't know what it was. She only knew she had to know.

A knock on the window startled her and she looked up to see her favorite librarian smiling at her.

Andrew Stargel opened her car door for her while she gathered her laptop, coffee, and notebook. He looked the same as he always did: a little disheveled, glasses falling down his nose, too large corduroy jacket almost falling off.

"You're early today, Ms. Constance. Haven't seen you in a while." He adjusted his messenger bag.

Andrew was only two years younger than Constance. She'd been trying to get him to drop the "Ms." for the last three, but his upbringing always won out.

"I know. I've been living in the pit of despair I call my office."

He smiled a lopsided grin at her. "How's the book comin' along?"

"Ink and paper groan when I reach for them now," she joked. "The book is on hiatus for now. I've been working on a few other projects that needed my attention." Constance closed her car door and walked with him up the old library steps.

"Well, hopefully, you'll get back to it soon enough." He unlocked the wide wooden door. The inset stained glass in the French doors had always been one of Constance's favorite parts of the library.

They walked in and the scent of books, old and new, floated over Constance. She took a deep breath and finally felt calm for the first time since before they left for the cemetery.

"Is there anything I can help you with today?" Andrew walked around the back of the wooden desk, that looked more like a bar, setting his keys and bag down on his chair.

"Actually, yes. I need whatever you have on Cane Creek Baptist Church."

Andrew visibly paled behind his stubble. The anxiety returned to her chest.

"I hate to tell you this, Ms. Constance, but there's not much." He moved to the door to the right of the desk that held the archives of the small Dahlonega town.

"We only know it was built after the Civil War." He moved to a filing cabinet and pulled out some old sheets of parchment, covered in plastic. "I can tell you a little about Cane Creek itself and the Reverend who started the church. We have the constitution from when the town was created. It was a mining community. Pretty simple folk, I guess."

Constance looked at the names written in erratic scrawls on the bottom of the page. "Five people from the Sheddle family and…one Stargel." She glanced up at Andrew.

"Yes ma'am. You know my family's been here a while."

"What about Sarah and Garland Gooch? Anything about them?"

Andrew narrowed his eyes at her but smiled. "You goin' on a ghost hunt, Ms. Constance?"

"Something like that. Why?"

"Sarah's one of the more famous ghosts around here. Her real name was Sarah Amelia Stargel, but everyone called her Emily."

A knot formed in Constance's stomach as he continued.

"Legends say she married Garland Gooch, got pregnant a few months later. He died before he could meet their baby, probably in a mining accident. Once the infant died, people said Emily was so heartbroken after

52

losing her husband and her baby, that she died too. Now she wanders around that cemetery humming lullabies to her infant."

Constance's heart clenched. If she'd lost any of her babies, she would probably do the same.

"But there's nothing about the church?"

"I think it'd be a good idea for you to stay away from that place." His eyes were intent with something Constance couldn't name. Maybe he wanted to protect her, but Constance wasn't letting this go easily.

"Can you just give me anything on Cane Creek? Or Emily? That should keep me busy today."

He searched her face for a long minute and Constance squirmed a little beneath his gaze. He finally nodded and returned to the filing cabinet. The stack of papers he pulled from a file marked Cane Creek was small. *This is going to be a dead end.*

Andrew handed them to her and then walked back out to his desk. Constance thumbed through them then remembered something he'd said.

"Wait. You said her maiden name was Stargel. So you're related to her, too?"

Andrew nodded as he swiveled the seat of his chair so he could sit down. "Yes, ma'am. It was my five-times Great Grandfather Stargel that helped settle Cane Creek. Emily was his daughter. So, I guess that makes her my many-times great aunt. Never really thought about it." He plopped in his chair and opened his computer.

"Just holler if you need anything."

Constance nodded then turned to the long table in the archives room to spread out and review all of the papers in the file.

A few hours later, she sipped her cold coffee and had learned precisely nothing about Cane Creek. There was a photo of the original church members and the original pastor, one J.J. Sheddle. He stood behind the pulpit of the church looking stern and missing an arm. How that had happened, she had no idea. The only other thing she'd been able to find from an old newspaper article was that the church hadn't gotten electricity until 1985.

Andrew had brought her the ghost stories book that Kristin had mentioned, but it had just repeated what Andrew had already told her. She did have a list of names from the original constitution, though. She'd looked through more archives from surrounding towns and newspaper articles, but it seemed these people lived pretty remotely in North Georgia in the 1850s and 60s and there wasn't much information on them.

Constance got up and stretched, then started organizing things on the table for Andrew to put back. He had his own system of cataloging the town's history and she didn't want to mess anything up.

He poked his head around the door a minute later. "Heard you moving around. Find what you needed?"

She glanced back at the papers. "Not at all." She checked her watch. "But I have to go meet the kids, so I guess I'll call it a day."

"Tell Lizzie that graphic novel she put on hold has come in."

Constance gathered her things, disappointed that she hadn't really made any progress in this search. She nodded and made her way to the door.

"Thanks for your help today."

"Such as it was," he shrugged. "If I think of anything else, I'll call you."

"Thanks," she mumbled.

The sky outside was bright in contrast to her mood, but the air was starting to turn chilly. Fall was just around the corner, and she had been looking forward to snuggling up under blankets and writing or reading.

Don't give up yet.

The voice she heard in her head wasn't hers. She looked around the parking lot thinking someone must have said something, but it was empty.

She got in her car and closed the door.

"I don't know where else to look," she said as much to herself as to whatever was talking to her.

An image of the church flashed into her mind's eye and she shivered.

She couldn't go back there. Not yet. There must be other records she could look into that would lead her anywhere but back there.

All Constance could see when she looked around her office was the looping handwriting that was so common in the 1860s. It'd been burned into her vision, even when she closed her eyes. She'd been staring at a roster of Civil War soldiers from North Georgia trying to make headway on…something. Something that might give her a clue as to who these men were. She could only remember the name of the man who had the big headstone: George Bruce. His headstone might not have had an actual date, but the confederate cross plaque in front of it had said 1861. There was no other conclusion she could come to other than the fact that he must have been a soldier. The trouble she'd run into was that there were several George Bruce's in Georgia at the time, and none listed Dahlonega

54

as their residence. She figured he must have been a man of some importance, but every time she thought she'd found something, it led to yet another dead end.

Constance's office door opened, and Lizzie came in with a plate of food and a glass of water. Constance glanced at her from behind her piles of notes but didn't stop reading.

"Mom? I brought you dinner." Lizzie leaned her hip against the desk. "When was the last time you ate?"

Constance glanced at the chicken, broccoli, and rice that steamed from the white ceramic plate. A pang of guilt stabbed her in the stomach. Her eldest child shouldn't have been having to take on the role of parent. She thought for a minute about Lizzie's question, but all she could remember was sitting where she had been.

"I...don't know. What's today?"

"Tuesday. August 16."

A week. I've lost a week? She remembered coming home from the library, making dinner and sitting down at her desk, but she'd been lost to research since then.

"I haven't seen you leave the office in a while. I thought I heard you upstairs in your room a few times, but mostly you've been in here."

"What about your brother and sister?"

"I've been taking them to school like I normally do. They say when they come home, you're usually asleep at your desk so they don't bother you."

"Have you been making dinner all week?"

"Yeah, but it's not a big deal. I got them pizza on Friday. I know how you get when you're deep into research, but I'm not sure I've ever seen you like this."

There was a soft rapping on the door and Kristin appeared in the doorway.

She was slow in her approach like she was meeting a caged tiger.

"I'm not going to bite, K."

"Good. You look like shit, though. When's the last time you bathed? I could smell you from outside."

Constance balled up a piece of paper and threw it at her. It smacked her right in the chest. Constance looked from her daughter to her best friend.

"So what is this? An intervention?"

Kristin's shoulders drooped. "We're just worried about you, Con. Lizzie called me and said she hasn't seen you emerge in a week. I've been calling and texting, too, with no answer. Sometimes it helps if you talk these things out when you're feeling stuck. How can we help?"

The pleading faces of her daughter and best friend looked down at her. She'd been so focused on finding answers—on tracing every genealogical record or Civil War soldier roster or mining record she could—that she'd forgotten about her family.

Her mouth pressed into a hard line. "You can't help. You don't understand and you won't listen."

"And you," she pointed an accusatory finger at Kristin, "don't remember anything anyway. What good are you?"

She turned away from them. She was being unreasonable, but she couldn't stop herself.

"All right, grumpy pants," Lizzie chided, "Get up. You're coming into the dining room to eat and then you're taking a shower. I'll force you into the tub if I have to."

"No, Lizzie," Constance pulled the arm that Lizzie tried to grab away. "I have to finish this."

"Finish what, mom?"

"I have to find out what happened to them." Constance didn't really even know if she was talking about George Bruce, the men, or the Gooch family, but it didn't even matter anymore.

"Well, you're useless to yourself and everyone else without food and sleep. So we're doing that first. These people have been dead for at least 160 years. I think they can wait a few more days."

Constance didn't argue again or pull away when Lizzie reached for her.

"Did you say it's August 16?" She asked Lizzie.

"Yeah, why?"

Tomorrow is her birthday. Constance immediately formed a new plan. She allowed herself to be ushered into her bathroom by Lizzie while Kristin followed along upstairs with the plate of food.

"Don't let her come down until she eats every bite," Lizzie charged to Kristin.

"Yes ma'am," Kristin saluted to her.

Lizzie closed the bathroom door behind her and Constance started to undress.

"You ever thought about getting that girl into the military after high school? She'd make a damn good officer." Kristin picked at the broccoli on Constance's plate then glanced over at her. "Damn, woman! You're all skin and bones. It really has been a while since you've eaten, hasn't it?"

Constance didn't say anything as she started the shower and got in. She let the heat skald her skin and turn her lobster-red while she thought about her next plan. Kristin tried to make small talk through the shower curtain, but Constance's mind was miles away. She pictured the church with its pristine white paint and the black numbers of the year on the front.

She'd been shown that this was the answer, but she didn't want to revisit that place. Especially not alone. Kristin wouldn't return with her. She couldn't take Lizzie. Maybe Andrew would go. His kin had settled the area. Maybe he'd be up for a ride. For her own peace of mind, she'd have to go in the daytime, though. And tomorrow was Emily's birthday. Spirits were known to be active on anniversary dates. Maybe she'd be able to get some guidance, some direction, from the woman herself.

The water and hair-washing ritual didn't soothe Constance in the way it should have. She felt that Emily's spirit was benign, but whatever was happening in the church didn't feel as friendly. However, maybe the church had an archive of its own. Maybe she could talk to the current pastor and he'd have some information about the history of the church that Andrew didn't know maybe she could find out what happened to Reverend Sheddle's arm maybe they'd have an answer for why Kristin's memory of the headstones had been erased after they drove through the fog maybe she—

"Con? You okay in there?"

Constance finished rinsing her hair. "Yeah, fine." Then turned off the shower.

Kristin handed her a towel then shoved the plate of food in her hands. "It's a little cold but eat it."

Constance tried not to roll her eyes. "Cold broccoli is a no. The rest I'll eat."

She toweled herself off, wrapped her robe around her, and wandered into her bedroom to eat on her bed.

Grady came bounding in a few minutes later. "Hi, momma! You feeling better?" He almost knocked the plate off of her lap and Constance wanted to yell at him. *Where is all of this anger coming from?* She barely managed to tamp it down.

She smiled at him as Meg came sashaying through the door, happy as a puppy.

"Momma!" Constance hugged her fiercely. Both of her children stood next to each other and smiled at her. She'd missed them. She placed one hand on the face of each of her Littles and looked into their dark blue eyes. They had her eyes: deep blue with a lighter blue around the iris. Grady had flecks of gray in his, and Constance had told him from the time he was a baby that it looked like he had snowflakes floating in them. They looked remarkably alike. And even though they were thirteen months apart, they acted more like twins. Meg joked that she had twin telepathy with her brother and said she could hear his thoughts on more than one occasion.

Constance rubbed her thumb over a scar on Grady's cheek that he'd gotten as a baby. Her other thumb over a set of freckles just under Meg's right eye.

You've been blessed with beautiful babies. You shouldn't have been.

The voice was back, but this time with malice. As she held her children's faces, they began to change. The flesh of their cheeks cooled and became sunken and pallid. Their eyes set deeper into their sockets. Grady's scar began to bleed fresh blood onto her thumb, while Meg's freckles seemed to melt down her cheek. Constance started to pull her hands away, and as she did, the flesh of their faces came with it. It landed with a *squelch* on the floor at her feet. In another breath, she saw only skulls with tufts of uneven golden hair still attached. Their teeth grimaced at her in deathly smiles, their eyes hollow.

Constance felt the scream stick in her throat.

"Momma? What's wrong?" Grady sounded concerned, but how could he be speaking when he had no tongue to do so?

"Grady, come on. Mama saw something bad. Let's go to bed. She needs to sleep."

Constance covered her mouth. *It can't be real.*

Kristin came around the other side of the bed. "Constance?"

Constance could feel her face frozen in fear and the tears that threatened to fall from her lashes. She searched Kristin's face, "My babies. What did they do to my babies?"

"Your babies are fine. Grady, Meg, and Lizzie are all fine. Healthy. They were just here, okay? Nothing is wrong."

Constance felt warm hands running up and down her arms and realized that her body was as cold as ice and her hands shook uncontrollably.

"Can you tell me what you saw?"

Constance could barely shake her head but as she did, she felt a hot tear fall onto her own cheek.

"Let's lay down. I'm going to give you a pill to help you sleep. Do you think you can swallow it?"

Constance didn't move. Didn't nod her head, but Kristin brought the water up to her lips anyway and pushed the pill in her mouth. Constance swallowed it and dutifully laid down. She was afraid if she closed her eyes, she'd see the image of her children's skulls again.

"Will you stay until I fall asleep?" Kristin had gone back to the other side of the bed and sat down next to her.

"Of course I will, sweetheart. Everything will be better in the morning."

She didn't see their faces when she closed her eyes. Instead, she saw the church again. But this time, the tendrils of fog dripped blood when they moved toward her.

Constance was awakened by bright light. It streamed into her bedroom and annoyed her. She didn't want to get up. Her head pounded and she felt groggy. She vaguely remembered Kristin giving her something to sleep. But the memory of her children's faces slammed into her memory and overshadowed everything else. She threw back the covers, headache forgotten, and got out of bed.

Something odd was under her feet. It felt gritty. When she looked down, she realized that someone had poured a salt circle around her bed. She reached a hand under her pillow and found one of her own pouches for dreamless sleep under it. She'd always kept a few made for Lizzie who sometimes struggled with nightmares. The lavender and rosemary wafted up to her as she rubbed it between her hands.

Sweet, but unnecessary. The thought was not her own.

She glanced down at the salt circle again. Something felt like it was pushing against her body, not allowing her to cross the circle, but she pushed back and crossed it just the same.

She ran down the hallway to Grady's room and found his bed empty. When she got to Meg's it was the same.

The scent of coffee wafted up from the kitchen and she made her way downstairs.

"Good morning, Sunshine," Kristin said from the dining room table. Her husband, William, sat next to her sipping a cup of coffee and munching on bacon.

"You look better this morning. Got some color back in your cheeks. Did you sleep okay?"

Constance nodded. "Where are the kids?"

Kristin glanced at William then back to Constance. "At school. It's Wednesday, remember?"

Wednesday. Emily's birthday. She needed to get to the church.

"What are y'all doing here?"

"I had the day off," William said around a mouthful of bacon. "We thought we'd spend it with you."

Constance walked over to the counter to pour herself a cup of coffee.

"I don't need one babysitter, let alone two, K."

"Dammit, Con," Kristin slammed her hand on the table and William tried to soothe her. "You're not okay. I'm not leaving you alone until you tell me what the hell is going on. Are you having some kind of nervous breakdown?"

"No. I don't have to tell you anything." Constance smiled over her coffee.

William glanced over at his wife. "I told you she wouldn't listen," he mumbled to her.

"Look. I don't know what happened after we left the cemetery, but you have to tell me something. Did something come back with you? This is not you! You don't neglect your children. You don't neglect our friendship. You're the most reliable, responsible person I've ever known."

Anger welled inside Constance's chest. She didn't owe anyone an explanation about anything. Especially when she didn't have any answers to give. She couldn't admit to anyone that all the time she'd been spending on this wild goose chase might have been for nothing.

Make them leave.

"How well can you ever truly know someone? Even someone you love?" She glanced over at William. "Apparently not well at all." Constance looked over at him pointedly. He pushed back from the table and walked out of the room. She heard the front door slam shut behind him.

Kristin pushed back her chair and made to follow him. "I hope whatever you're doing is worth all of this…loss." And she stormed out after her husband.

She was glad to be rid of their presence. Constance glided to her office, looking for her cell phone. She finally found it under a stack of papers. It was dead. She plugged it into the charger in the kitchen, then picked up the receiver of the vintage phone she kept in the kitchen.

She dialed the number of the library that she knew by heart. It rang twice before Andrew picked up.

"Andrew. I need a favor. Can you get away for a little while today?"

"I still think this is a really bad idea," Andrew said as they pulled up to the church later that afternoon. Andrew had called a few people who knew the current pastor at the church. He'd finally gotten in touch with him and made an appointment to meet him at 4.

Constance had met the Littles getting off their bus, patted them hesitantly on the head, told Lizzie she'd had an errand to run, and ran out the door to pick Andrew up before Lizzie had even gotten all the way out of her car.

"It's just research. When is that ever a bad idea?" Constance had barely looked at him during the twenty-minute ride. After seeing her children desiccate before her the night before, she was afraid to look anyone in the eye. William and Kristin had been an exception this morning, but in her anger she hadn't been able to do anything else.

She was still unsure if that had been a premonition or not, but the pull in her chest for knowledge remained and thrummed deeper in her veins right next to the ever-present anxiety that now she might also have to save her children.

Her palms were slick on the steering wheel as they pulled into the church parking lot. The church looked much less menacing and almost inviting in the daylight.

A man waited for them in the doorway and smiled as they approached.

Andrew extended his hand in greeting, "Reverend Sheddle, thank you for meeting us this afternoon."

Nausea rolled in Constance's stomach. The man in front of her looked younger than the photo she'd seen of the now-deceased Reverend Sheddle from the 1860s-era photo but other than that, she could have been looking at the same man. Right down to the missing left arm.

The grin he turned to Constance looked far from warm. "Please," he gestured them both into the small sanctuary.

As soon as she crossed the threshold, Constance knew she was in a place she didn't belong. The one-room church had dark, wood-paneled walls. Gold chandeliers were evenly spaced on the ceiling, and she counted them to prevent herself from turning and running. There were eight. She counted them again and walked to the simple pulpit at the front of the church. The lights were off, but the opened shades allowed enough sunlight in that she could see the simplicity of the church well enough.

As she turned around to take in the rest of the church, she saw the wall that Kristin had described. Along the back wall were several marks on either side of the door that could only be called scratches. It looked like the fingernails that had dug in had desperately tried to claw their way out. Even from a slight distance, Constance could see that some looked deep and others superficial. They should have been easy to cover with new paneling, but instead, they stood out sharply against the dark wood.

She ran a thumb over her own fingernails to steady her heartbeat.

"How can I help you, folks?" The Reverend sat down on the front pew and adjusted his pants before looking up at Andrew.

Andrew glanced at Constance, but she couldn't answer. She was staring at the Reverend.

"We were, uh, hoping you could tell us about the history of the church. We've looked through the archives in the library but couldn't find much."

"Oh, I see." The Reverend seemed thoughtful. "For what purpose, if I might ask?"

Andrew cleared his throat. "Ms. Constance is working on a book inspired by the area."

The current Reverend Sheddle turned his attention to Constance. She met his gaze and saw no warmth, no real life behind his gold-rimmed glasses.

"What an endeavor for a young lady like yourself," the tip of his mouth quirked up in an emotionless smile.

"Unfortunately, we don't keep written records of the church, its history, or our congregants. Not any that we'd share for public consumption at any rate. We're a humble and simple congregation and have been since our founding in 1866. We overcame the War between the States and some other troubles and have been serving the spiritual needs of Cane Creek since then. That's about all I can tell you."

Constance's ears perked up and she spoke for the first time since arriving. "Other troubles?"

The Reverend sat back and crossed his legs. "This area tended to be full of uncouth heathens." He considered Andrew. "That was one of the reasons the original Reverend Sheddle and your kin started a church in this area back then. It was a necessary evil, but one he took on with the vigor and enthusiasm of a man who loved the Lord and wanted to serve his flock."

Constance took a step closer. "You mean the Indigenous population?"

His dark gaze turned to Constance once again. "No, ma'am. I mean witches."

Like you.

The voice rang in her head like a tuning fork had been set off.

The image of a hanging tree swam in her vision, and she had to put out a hand to steady herself.

You don't belong here.

When her vision cleared, Constance met the Reverend's gaze once again. Fog was beginning to pour into the closed windows and the buzzing she'd heard on the night she and Kristin drove through it was returning. She glanced at Andrew, but he didn't seem to see anything out of the ordinary, because while he looked concerned for her faltering, he didn't seem to be seeing what she was.

Constance knew that this would be the last opportunity she had for answers. She was sure the Reverend wouldn't be so welcoming if she came back.

She swallowed the bile that was rising in her throat and shook her head against the buzz.

"Surely you must know some of the names of the women the original congregants murdered."

He looked taken aback, but the Reverend maintained his relaxed posture. "Do you have children?"

Constance nodded.

"But no wedding ring, I see. How sad for them. Marriage is a sacred vow in the eyes of the Lord. Even unto death."

He picked at an invisible piece of lint on his knee. "I am endowed with protecting my congregation, ma'am. The members now and the ones who have come before us. And I imagine you would do anything to protect your children wouldn't you?"

The image of her skeletal children slammed into her again and this time Constance's knees did go weak, and she bent over to catch her breath.

Andrew slipped an arm around her waist and put another on her arm to steady her.

"I think we need to go, Ms. Constance. You don't look well at all."

Constance didn't respond but allowed herself to be led toward the car. Andrew turned at the still-open front door and turned back to the Reverend.

"Thank you for your time, sir."

"You're welcome back to our Sunday services, anytime. Especially you, ma'am. We'll keep you in our prayers and hope you feel better."

Andrew closed the door behind them, but Constance noticed that the fog lapped at their heels the whole way to the car.

Constance had broken the salt ring around her bed after a much-needed nap. She couldn't explain anything to Andrew as he'd driven her home. He lived less than a mile away and had told her he'd be fine to walk home and she needn't trouble herself about him.

She'd made dinner mindlessly and let the children chatter to her about their day, but she was elsewhere. The effort of being present with them was overwhelming. She needed a new plan.

The Reverend was clearly warning her to stay away, but had the voice she'd been hearing been his or someone else's? The only real way to know was to try to get answers from her last lead and she'd been dead for some time.

After she tucked the Littles into bed and made sure that Lizzie was asleep, she packed a bag and left a note for her children.

It was almost eleven by the time she got to the cemetery. The moon was new and dark and didn't illuminate anything the way it had done only two weeks before. Still, she'd parked as close to Emily's grave as she could, gathered her things, and tamped down her nerves as she walked through the headstones.

She was pulled to the grave by a tugging in her chest. She wouldn't have needed her flashlight or her memory to help guide her.

She knelt in the middle of the family plot, already overgrown again, and set out four candles, one for each of the cardinal directions, around her. She pulled the salt from her bag and enclosed herself, the headstones, and the candles within it. The pouch of various herbs and crystals was safely hidden in her pocket.

She heard humming from behind her as she touched the match to the side of the matchbox. She didn't know how she knew the song, but she hummed along as she struck the match and bent to light the first candle. The flame went out as soon as she touched it to the wick.

"Come now, Sister. You don't need all of this." The voice that had spoken was musical and young. It was also in front of her now.

Constance looked up, still holding her match. "Sister?"

The woman in front of her was as real as anyone she'd ever seen. Her hair fell to her waist in dark auburn waves. Her face was still round like childhood hadn't left her completely, but the body underneath her black dress said differently. Her corset gave her an hourglass figure and her skirt fell around wide hips. Her eyes glowed an ethereal gray in the darkness.

She sat on top of Emily's headstone and flounced her skirt around her. "We're kindred spirits, you and I."

Constance dropped the match, the candles forgotten. "Tell me what happened to you. To these men."

"Took you long enough to get up the gumption to ask."

"I wasn't sure you'd tell me."

"If you'da brought that man back with you, I wouldn't have."

"Why not?"

"Because he has to die. He's one of them."

"Andrew? No. He's your great-nephew."

"And my brother was the one who placed the noose around my neck." Emily snapped. "Bein' kin means nothin'."

"I don't understand."

"Then I'll tell you a story. A long time ago, my mama and grandmama were healers. Grandmama was the daughter of the Creek people. They didn't and never would believe in no Christian God," she spat on the ground. "And neither would I. Grandmama said Mama believed in nature, in the gifts given from the earth. She made medicines, she birthed babies, saw sickness come and go. People came to her for help."

"I tried to be good like her, I promise I did, but I just...couldn't." Emily ran her finger in the dirt in circles.

"What happened to her?"

"I killed her coming out of her. Grandmama raised us."

"What happened to your husband?"

Emily stopped and turned her head to look at her through the hair that had fallen in her face. "I helped him meet his maker," she said with a grin. "He thought I might suddenly decide to take God into my heart after we

65

married. Poor bastard. I loved him, too." She twirled her hair around a finger and looked at his headstone. "But you know all about killing husbands, don't you?"

"I didn't kill my husband."

"You took his children from him. You might as well have."

Constance shook her head. She wasn't responsible for what had happened. Her therapist, her family, her children reminded her of that as often as she needed to hear it.

"This isn't about me."

Emily hopped off the headstone and landed on her knees in front of Constance. A cold hand reached up and tried to touch her cheek. Emily cocked her head as she looked into Constance's eyes.

"Oh, but it is, dear Sister."

Constance couldn't help but stare back into the glowing eyes in front of her. So many emotions churned within them.

"And your child?"

Constance sighed and sat up straight, removing her hand. "Yes, my poor baby child. She was sickly when she was born. The good Reverend took her from me because they suspected I'd killed her papa and they wanted to *pray* over her. She died mysteriously soon after. They had a horseshit trial a week later," she gestured to her headstone, "and I've been here ever since. I sing to my baby because it's the only kind voice she ever heard in a world full of monsters. It makes her happy."

Emily looked over Constance's shoulder and scooted closer to her, their knees touching in the circle.

"We have to hurry. They're coming."

Constance glanced behind her. The fog was creeping up the hill, undulating and swirling on top of itself.

"Who is?"

"Them." Emily nodded to the headstones around them. "I bound them. Not everyone can see, you know. You and your friend did. They made her forget. Too bad she's not really your blood. I could have used her, too. But…you're more powerful than you know. Mr. George and them tried to stop you."

Constance felt a chill in her fingertips like she'd stuck them in a bucket of ice. When she looked down, she could see Emily's hands over hers.

"It's a shame. You should have listened."

"What are you doing?" Constance could hear the buzzing behind her growing louder.

"I've waited almost 200 years for someone to help me stop them. You've been looking for answers…but the answer is you."

Constance felt the chill creeping deeper into her body. As it did, Emily's appearance grew fainter and fainter. A tightness started building in Constance's body making her limbs go ridged as her heart and mind tried to fight against this intruder. Images of a life that wasn't hers flashed in her memory: The knife that slid across a man's neck in the lamplight. The pains of a hard labor. Watching a man with a pillow stifle the shrill cries of an infant. The rough twine of a noose cutting off all oxygen. Anger and despair building for generations.

Constance closed her eyes against the onslaught of the anguish.

She felt the warmth of the fog encircle her wrists, pulling at her, but when she opened her eyes again, it shrank back from her as if it'd been burned. Her vision glowed gray and blue around her and the fog left crimson stains on the hillside and headstones as it receded.

"Now we begin in earnest," she said to the empty hill.

WE WANT TO HEAR FROM YOU!

Reviews are the best way to communicate with us as a company. ArrowHeart wants to know how our stories made you feel and did you enjoy the way they were laid out. Praise and constructive criticism are welcome!

You can leave reviews for us on Amazon, Goodreads, and other websites. We thank you for your purchase and hope that these stories left something with you. If you'd like to submit or purchase the next volume look for more information on our website at:

www.arrowheartpublishing.com

Thanks again!

www.ingramcontent.com/pod-product-compliance
Lightning Source LLC
Chambersburg PA
CBHW030516130626
46549CB00007B/3011